W9-COI-770

How to Become a Perfect Knight

in Five Days!

Text by Pierrette Dubé

Illustrations by Caroline Hamel

alphabet
soup

an imprint of
WINDMILL BOOKS
New York

Published in 2010 by Windmill Books, LLC
303 Park Avenue South, Suite # 1280, New York, NY 10010-3657

Adaptations to North American Edition © 2010 Windmill Books

Original title: Comment devenir un parfait chevalier en 5 jours
Original Publisher: Les éditions Imagine inc
© Pierrette Dubé / Caroline Hamel 2008
© Les éditions Imagine inc. 2008
English text © Les éditions Imagine inc 2008

Back Cover art by Luc Melanson

Publisher Cataloging in Publication

Dubé, Pierrette, 1952-
        How to become a perfect knight in five days. – North American ed. / text by Pierrette Dubé; illustrations by Caroline Hamel
p.   cm. – (Rainy day readers)
Summary: When young Philbert Metalblade is sent to the Academy for Apprentice Knights, he uses his own inventions to accomplish the feats a knight must complete.
ISBN 978-1-60754-373-2 (lib.) – ISBN 978-1-60754-374-9 (pbk.)
ISBN 978-1-60754-375-6 (6-pack)
        1. Knights and knighthood—Juvenile fiction   2. Inventions—Juvenile fiction
[1. Knights and knighthood—Fiction   2. Inventions—Fiction]   I. Hamel, Caroline
II. Title   III. Series
        [Fic]—dc22

Printed in the United States of America

For more great fiction and nonfiction, go to windmillbooks.com.

To Simon and Benoît, who, fortunately, are not perfect knights.

Pierrette Dubé

A knight full of great ideas for my adorable little princess.

Caroline Hamel

hilbert Metalblade was born the youngest in a long line of knights, who were known throughout the land for their bravery and fighting skills. His ancestors defended kings and won numerous battles. They were all muscular, solidly built, and were as tall as giants.

Philbert was different than his family members; he was smaller and had a unique personality all his own. He wasn't as colossal as his Uncle Amos or solid and muscular like his Uncle Horace. He wasn't as quick-tempered as his Uncle Ludovic or as bold and daring as his Uncle Henry. And of course, he didn't dream of war like his Uncle Aldabert.

"This child is too small," cried his father, the Great Dagobert. "But what is even more frightening is his good temper."

In the Metalblade family, no one had seen anyone like Philbert in centuries.

AMOS

ADALBERT

LUDOVIC

HORACE

HENRI

Little Philbert was a dreamer with lots of imagination. Instead of playing with swords he would spend his hours designing and building contraptions no one had seen before. His inventions seemed odd to his father who couldn't understand why Philbert would want to spend his time on such things.

"When will you stop dreaming?" complained his father. "A good knight should know how to fight, not spend all his time constructing strange devices."

How much the Great Dagobert wished Philbert was like his cousin "Break-Metal", who was well on his way toward becoming a future knight!

But Philbert had other hobbies that he found much more interesting.

"In the end", he told himself. "I don't have to be tall to walk like a giant."

"What should I do?" Great Dagobert asked his father and most trusted adviser.

"We have to give him a horse" recommended old Norbert. "Without a horse, he'll never be a knight."

And so Philbert got a horse for his birthday. The very first time he got in the saddle, he sneezed, once, twice, ten times! Much to his father's disappointment, Philbert was allergic to horses!

The castle doctor prescribed a potion to help Philbert stop sneezing, but even with that, Philbert just wasn't interested. He preferred getting around by another type of transportation, one he had invented himself.

"What should I do?" wailed the Great Dagobert.

"We must send him to the Academy for Apprentice Knights", suggested grandfather Norbert, while handing him a brochure.

In all of the Metalblade family history no one had ever needed to go to school to learn to be a knight, it was just something that came naturally. But in Philbert's case, it was necessary.

ACADEMY FOR APPRENTICE KNIGHTS

Become a Perfect Knight in

5 Days!

or your money back

On Monday morning, Philbert left for the Academy. He brought several bags and parcels, which contained his tools and the materials needed for working on his many inventions.

When he arrived, the schoolyard was full of huge boys that towered above Philbert. The biggest boy of all was Caligula Bigarms, a child that seemed as well suited for war as Philbert's cousin Break-Metal.

"Today", announced Professor Lofty-Britches, "you will learn to climb a wall, a task every perfect knight must accomplish with agility."

As the apprentice knights grasped their ladders, Caligula Bigarms began to climb first.

Philbert figured getting over the wall would be much simpler with a pole.

However, he should've calculated the landing better...

On Tuesday Professor Stands-at-Attention announced, "Today you will learn to wear your armor, helmet, and shield with dignity, like all perfect knights."

Caligula Bigarms' armor fitted him like a glove. To Philbert, the gear seemed a little cumbersome. After making some modifications, he created a way to dart between enemies, which caused a commotion...

On Wednesday, Professor Stabs-a-Lot announced, "Today you will learn to handle a sword and spear with dexterity, as all perfect knights must learn to do."

Of course Caligula Bigarms was very talented at this task, while Philbert thought the swords and spears were too dangerous. With some modifications, Philbert created a less sharp and much more refreshing weapon to use.

Professor Stabs-a-Lot didn't really appreciate his efforts…

On Thursday Professor Side-Saddle said, "Today we will learn to ride horses, because perfect knights are, above all, excellent riders."

Unfortunately Philbert forgot to bring his allergy potion. During the lesson he disappeared without explanation. Everyone looked, but he was nowhere to be found.

With one day left before graduation, everyone was eager to master the final task necessary for becoming a perfect knight. All of the apprentice knights' families were coming. Even the king and queen were invited to the graduation ceremony!

"What will my father, grandfather, and the entire Metalblade family think if I don't get my diploma as a perfect knight?" worried Philbert.

Philbert had a plan. He stayed up all night to complete his invention in time.

The next day everyone met at the Academy's sports field. "For your final task today," announced the principal, Professor Bombastic, "You will learn to face danger head-on, like proper knights. You will have to travel to a cave where a fearsome dragon called Burn-Your-Bones-to-a-Crisp lives. You must face him and bring back a piece of his treasure."

At that moment, Philbert appeared at the starting line on a strange-looking machine, which stunned and puzzled the audience.

"What has my son invented this time?" cried out the Great Dagobert melodramtically.

The apprentice knights, with Caligula Bigarms in the lead, took off at a full gallop. Philbert did the same but on a…?

At the dragon's cave the attackers' seemed to make the dragon sneeze.

"Oh tar and feathers!" cried out Burn-Your-Bones-to-a-Crisp, "I can tell there are horses nearby!"

He sneezed once, twice, ten times! Philbert figured out that the dragon was also allergic to horses…

"Good!" he said. "With the metal frame of my invention, I'll be able to get closer to the dragon than the apprentices riding horses."

Now, Burn-Your-Bones-to-a-Crisp wasn't brought up with good manners and no one had ever taught him to cover his mouth before he sneezed… "Aaaahhhh-choo!"

With the dragon blowing soot and flames everywhere, the apprentice knights were frightened and backed away (Caligula Bigarms was the first). Philbert was able to slip through the cave's entrance without being noticed.

To Professor Bombastic's despair, all of the apprentice knights returned to the sports field empty-handed. All except for . . . Philbert.

"Where did he go?" wondered the Great Dagobert. "I hope the dragon didn't burn him to a crisp!"

The guests were starting to get restless when suddenly Philbert appeared waving a medallion studded with rubies.

The crowd exploded with applause.

Professor Bombastic was irritated that the Academy's worst pupil had won the final competition and, in spite of the crowds' protest he decided that Philbert was disqualified for riding "an unauthorized animal".

Dagobert Metalblade, however, couldn't have been prouder.

"That's my son, Philbert!" he boasted. "The child is pure genius!"

"It is true", thought grandfather Norbert, "that Metalblades have always been knights, but an inventor is also an honorable profession..."

Later that night, the Great Dagobert was curious about how Philbert handled the dragon and asked:

"Tell me son, how did you manage to vanquish the dragon and rob him of his medallion?"

"It was simple", answered Philbert. "In exchange for the medallion, I promised him my next invention."